USBORNE

FIRST THOUSAND WORDS
IN ENGLISH

Heather Amery

Illustrated by Stephen Cartwright

Edited by Nicole Irving
and designed by Andy Griffin

On every big picture across two pages,
there is a little yellow duck to look for.
Can you find it?

About this book

All young children will enjoy this exciting picture word book. Parents and teachers sharing it with them will discover that each page provides lively situations to explore, and to talk and laugh about.

The First Thousand Words is designed to be used at many different levels, so that children of various ages and abilities will find it stimulating and amusing.

At its easiest level, the book can be used as a picture word book for looking and talking. As they grow familiar with favorite pages, children will be able to describe and give names to pictures. Gradually, they can be introduced to the printed words, and, with help and encouragement, they will soon begin matching words with pictures.

Older children can use this book when writing their own stories. It will provide them with ideas, new words and correct spellings.

There is a word list at the back of the book, which brings together all the words in alphabetical order. It can be used to encourage children to look up words and find the right page and picture. This is an important skill, which will prepare children to use simple information books and dictionaries.

Remember, this is a book of a thousand words. It will take time to learn them all!

About this revised edition

This edition brings new life to an enormously popular book. The book has been redesigned to give even clearer pictures and labels, and there are many brand-new illustrations by Stephen Cartwright. The book has also been brought up to date, so that it now includes objects which have made their way into children's everyday lives in recent years.

At home

bed

bathtub

soap

faucet

toilet paper

toothbrush

water

toilet

sponge

sink

shower

bathroom

living room

towel

toothpaste

radio

cushion

CD

carpet

sofa

4

chair

comforter

comb

sheet

rug

closet

pillow

chest of drawers

mirror

brush

lamp

pictures

coat rack

telephone

bedroom

hall

radiator

video

newspaper

table

letters

stairs

5

The kitchen

refrigerator

glasses

clock

stool

teaspoons

light switch

laundry detergent

key

door

sink

vacuum cleaner

saucepans

forks

apron

ironing board

trash

kettle

knives

mop

dust cloth

tiles

broom

washing machine

dustpan

drawer

saucers

frying pan

stove

spoons

plates

iron

closet

dish towel

cups

matches

brush

bowls

The yard

wheelbarrow

beehive

snail

bricks

pigeon

shovel

ladybug

trash can

seeds

shed

watering can

worm

flowers

sprinkler

hoe

wasp

bee

trowel

bone

hedge

fork

lawn mower

path

leaves

tree

smoke

caterpillar

rake

bird's nest

sticks

grass

baby buggy

ladder

bonfire

garden hose

greenhouse

The workshop

screws

vise

sandpaper

drill

ladder

saw

sawdust

calendar

tool box

screwdriver

board

shavings

pocketknife

10

tacks

spider

bolts

nuts

cobweb

barrel

fly

ax

tape measure

hammer

file

paint can

plane

wood

nails

workbench

jars

11

The street

store

hole

café

ambulance

pavement

antenna

chimney

roof

bulldozer

bus

hotel

man

police car

pipes

drill

school

playground

12

taxi

crosswalk

factory

truck

traffic lights

movie theater

van

steamroller

trailer

house

market

steps

motorcycle

bicycle

fire engine

policeman

car

woman

lamp post

apartments

13

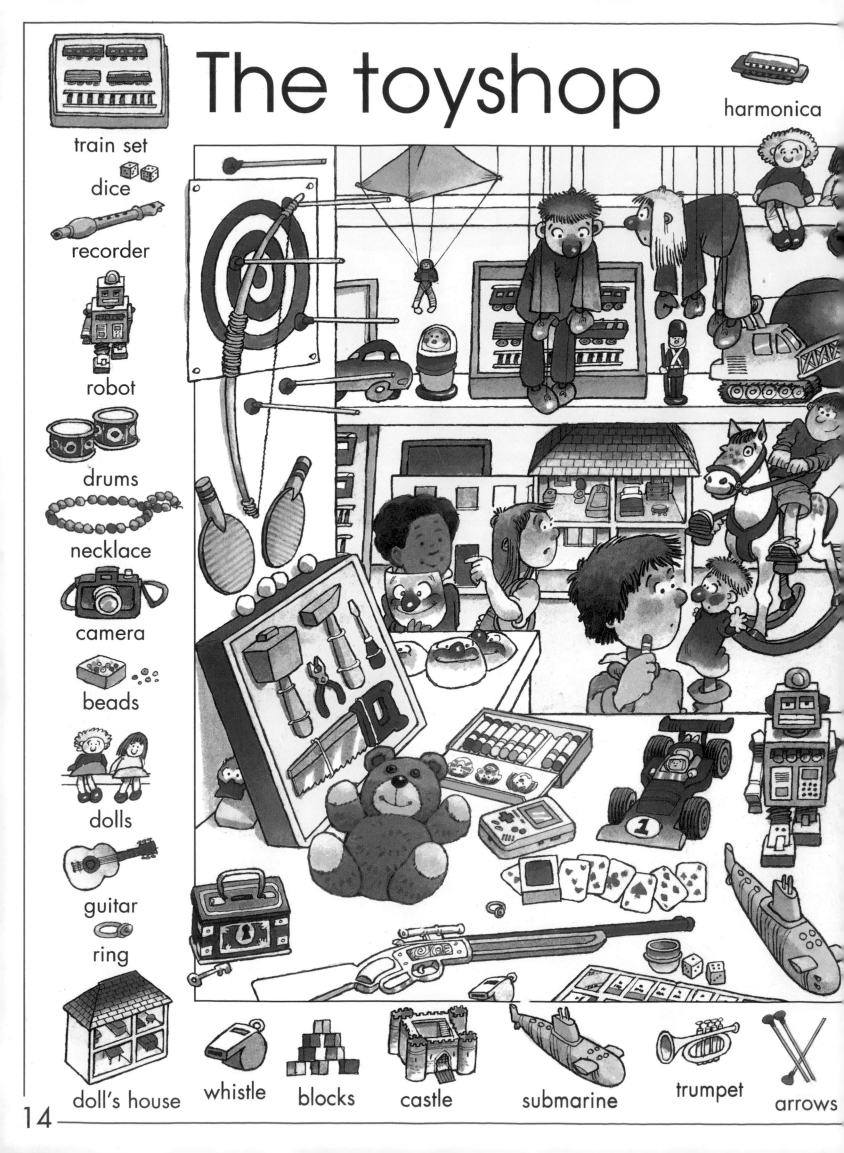

The toyshop

train set

dice

recorder

robot

drums

necklace

camera

beads

dolls

guitar

ring

doll's house

harmonica

whistle

blocks

castle

submarine

trumpet

arrows

bow parachute boat face paints steamroller masks

racing car

rocking horse

bank

marbles

puppets

piano

spacemen

crane clay gun soldiers paints rocket

15

The park

swings

bench

sandpit

picnic

kite

ice cream

dog

gate

path

frog

slide

tadpoles

lake

roller blades

bush

baby

skateboard

dirt

stroller

seesaw

children

tricycle

birds

fence

ball

boat

string

puddle

ducklings

jump-rope

trees

flower bed

swans

leash

ducks

The zoo

panda

wing

eagle

hippopotamus

bat

gorilla

paws

kangaroo

monkey

tail

wolf

iceberg

penguin

crocodile

bear

feathers

pelican

ostrich

dolphin

giraffe

lion

cubs

horns —

deer

camel

seal

polar bear

tortoise

trunk

rhinoceros

bison

elephant

beaver

zebra

snake

goat

shark

whale

tiger

leopard

19

Travel

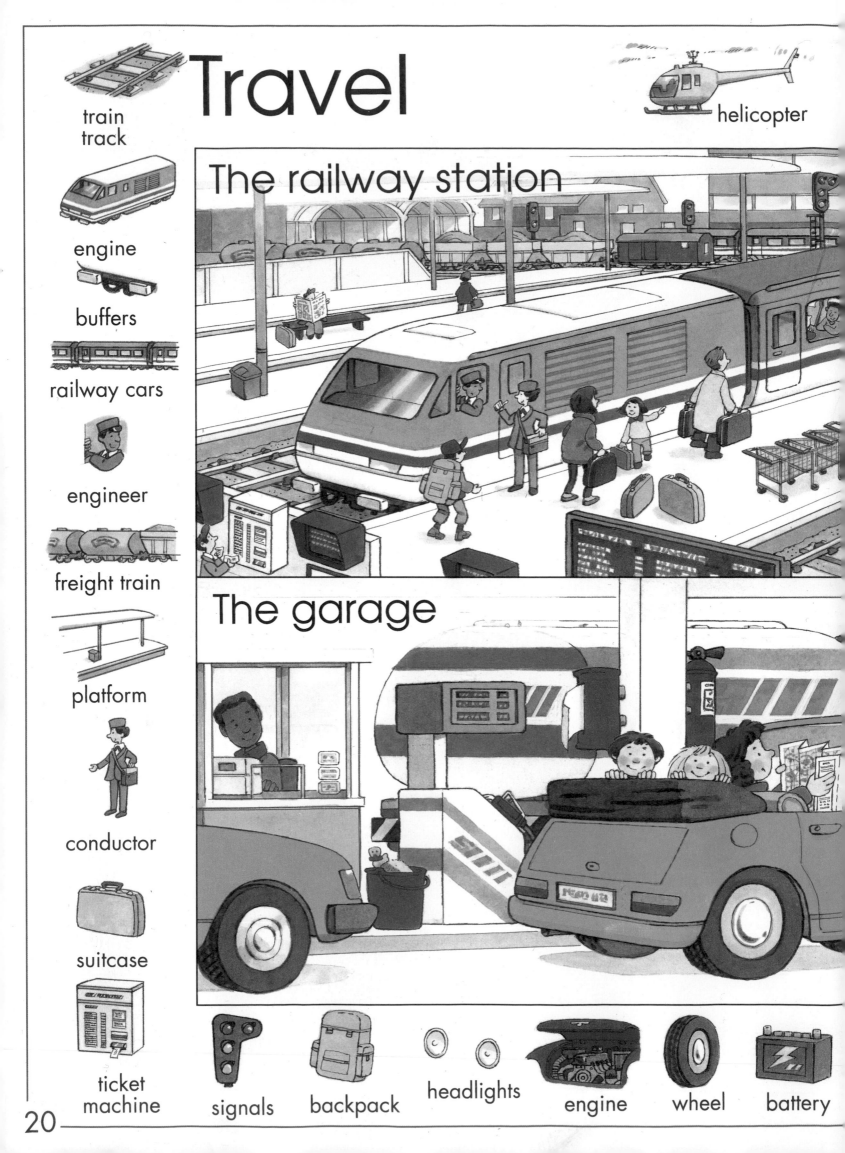

train track

engine

buffers

railway cars

engineer

freight train

platform

conductor

suitcase

ticket machine

helicopter

The railway station

The garage

signals

backpack

headlights

engine

wheel

battery

The airport

plane

flight attendant

runway

control tower

flight attendant

pilot

car wash

trunk

gas

tow truck

car wash

tanker

wrench

tire

hood

oil

gas pump

21

The country

windmill

mountain

hot-air balloon

butterfly

lizard

stones

fox

stream

signpost

porcupine

lock

squirrel

forest

badger

river

road

22

tents

canal

logs

town

moth

bridge

barge

waterfall

owl

tunnel

fox cubs

mole

fisherman

rocks

toad

train

camper

hill

23

The farm

haystack

sheepdog

ducks

lambs

pond

chicks

hayloft

pigsty

bull

ducklings

hen house

tractor

rooster

geese

tanker

barn

mud

cart

farmer

field

hens

calf

fence

saddle

cowshed

cow

plow

orchard

stable

piglets

shepherdess

turkeys

scarecrow

hay

sheep

straw bales

horse

pigs

farmhouse

25

The seaside

shell

sailboat

sea

oar

lighthouse

shovel

bucket

starfish

sandcastle

umbrella

flag

sailor

crab

seagull

island

motorboat

water-skier

waves

sunhat

cliff

ship

kayak

rope

pebbles

seaweed

net

paddle

fishing boat

flippers

donkey

fish

swimsuit

oil tanker

beach

rowboat

beach chair

27

At school

scissors

$$2 + 2 = 4$$
$$3 + 2 = 5$$

sums

eraser

ruler

photographs

felt-tip pens

thumbtacks

paints

boy

pencil

board

desk

books

pen

glue

chalk

drawing

wastepaper basket

teacher

box

map

brush

ceiling

wall

floor

notebook

alphabet

badge

aquarium

paper

blind

door handle

plant

globe

girl

crayons

lamp

easel

a b c d e f g
h i j k l m n
o p q r s t u
v w x y z

2+2=4
3+2=5

nurse

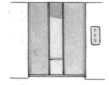

cotton balls

medicine

elevator

bathrobe

crutches

pills

tray

watch

thermometer

curtain

The hospital

teddy bear

apple

cast

bandage

wheelchair

jigsaw

doctor

syringe

The doctor

slippers

computer

adhesive bandage

banana

grapes

basket

toys

pear

cards

diaper

walking stick

television   nightgown   pajamas   orange   tissues   comic   waiting room

The party

presents

balloon

chocolate

candy

window

fireworks

ribbon

cake   straw   candle   paper chains   toys

32

tangerine

salami

cassette tape

sausage

chips

costumes

cherry

fruit juice

raspberry

strawberry

bulb

sandwich

butter

cookie

cheese

bread

tablecloth

The store

grapefruit

carrot

cauliflower

leek

mushroom

cucumber

lemon

celery

apricot

melon

grocery sack

cheese

fruit and vegetables

onion

cabbage

peach

lettuce

peas

tomato

eggs

plum

flour

scales

jars

meat

pineapple

yogurt

basket

bottles

purse

coin purse

money

cans

potatoes

spinach

beans

checkout

pumpkin

cart

Food

breakfast

lunch or dinner

coffee

boiled egg

fried egg

toast

jam

cream

milk

cereal

hot chocolate

sugar

honey

salt

pepper

tea

teapot

pancakes

rolls

supper or dinner

ham

soup

omelette

salad

chopsticks

hamburger

chicken

rice

ketchup

spaghetti

mashed potatoes

pizza

french fries

dessert

Me

head

hair

face

eyebrow

eye

nose

cheek

mouth

lips

teeth

tongue

chin

arm

elbow

tummy

ears

neck

shoulders

toes

foot

leg

knee

chest

back

bottom

hand

thumb

fingers

My clothes

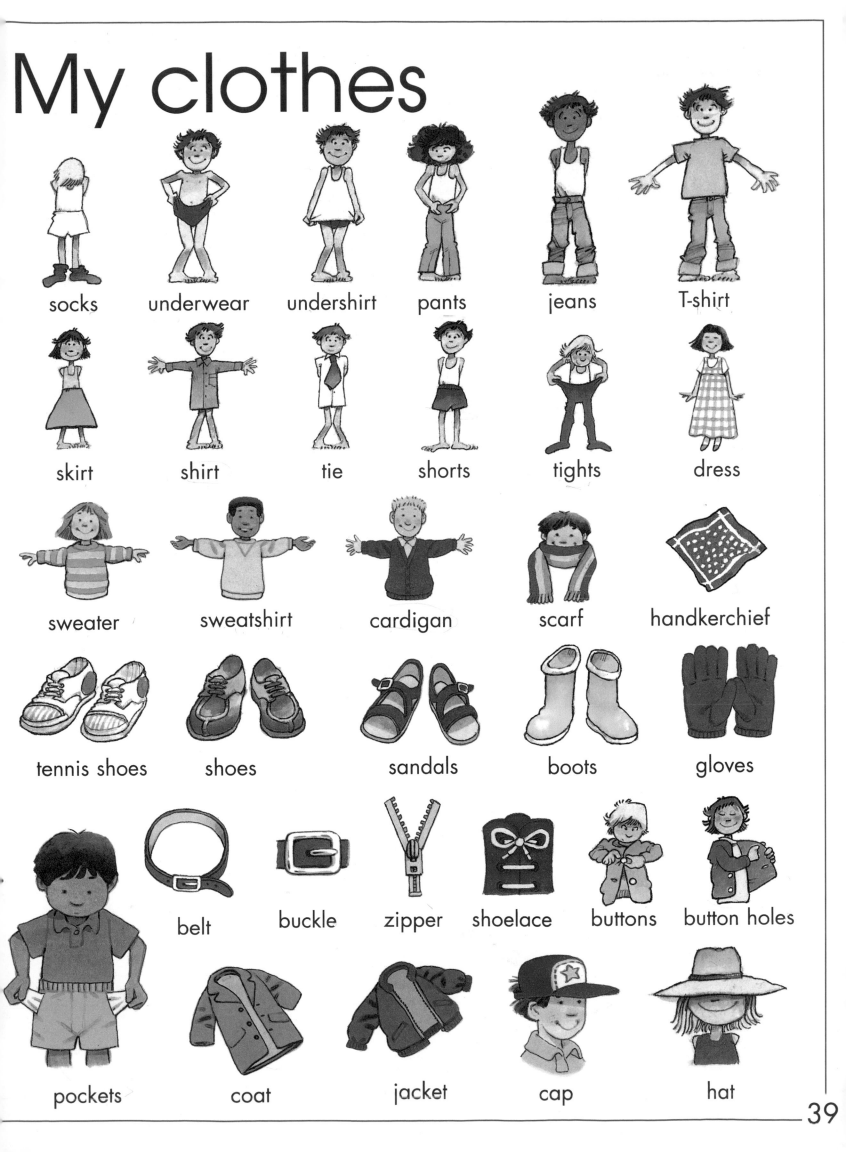

socks

underwear

undershirt

pants

jeans

T-shirt

skirt

shirt

tie

shorts

tights

dress

sweater

sweatshirt

cardigan

scarf

handkerchief

tennis shoes

shoes

sandals

boots

gloves

belt

buckle

zipper

shoelace

buttons

button holes

pockets

coat

jacket

cap

hat

People

chef

dancers

actor   actress

singers

astronaut

butcher

policeman

policewoman

carpenter

fireman

artist

judge

mechanics

barber

truck driver

bus driver

waiter   waitress

mail carrier

dentist

frogman

painter

baker

Families

aunt   uncle

son   daughter   mother   father
brother   sister   wife   husband

cousin

grandfather

grandmother

41

Doing things

laugh

smile

cry

think

listen

catch

throw

break

paint

write

chop

cut

eat

talk

dig

carry

drink

make

jump

crawl

dance

wash

knit

play

watch

climb

take

skip

fight

sleep

sew

wait

cook

hide

read

buy

push

sing

blow

pull

sweep

pick

fall

walk

run

sit

43

Opposite words

good

bad

far

near

cold

hot

wet

dry

top

bottom

over

under

dirty   clean

fat   thin

small   big

open   closed

few   many

first   last

left

44

out

in

easy

difficult

empty

full

soft

hard

front

high

slow

fast

back

low

long

short

dead

alive

dark

light

old

upstairs

right

new

downstairs

45

Days

Monday
Tuesday
Wednesday
Thursday
Friday
Saturday
Sunday

calendar

morning

evening

sun

night

space

moon

star

planet

spaceship

telescope

Special days

birthday

present

candle

birthday card

birthday cake

vacation

wedding day

bridesmaid

bride   bridegroom

camera

photographer

Christmas Day

reindeer

sleigh

Santa Claus

Christmas tree

Weather

sun

clouds

sky

umbrella

rain

lightning

fog

snow

dew

wind

mist

frost

rainbow

Seasons

spring

summer

autumn

winter

Pets

hamster

vet

guinea pig

kennel

puppy

dog

parakeet

food

parrot

beak

rabbit

canary

cage

cat

basket

mouse

kitten

milk

goldfish

Sports and exercise

basketball

rowing

snowboarding

sailing

windsurfing

racket

cricket

karate

tennis

football

gym

bat

ball

fishing rod

dance

baseball

fishing

bait

rugby

diving

swimming pool

race

swimming

archery

target

hang-gliding

helmet

jogging

cycling

climbing

judo

horse

pony

locker

soccer

riding

changing room

badminton

table tennis

ice skates

ice-skating

ski pole

chairlift

ski

skiing

sumo wrestling

51

Colors

orange

green

black

gray

red

brown

pink

white   blue   purple   yellow

Shapes

diamond

cone

rectangle

circle

star

cube

oval

triangle

square

crescent

Numbers

1	one	
2	two	
3	three	
4	four	
5	five	
6	six	
7	seven	
8	eight	
9	nine	
10	ten	
11	eleven	
12	twelve	
13	thirteen	
14	fourteen	
15	fifteen	
16	sixteen	
17	seventeen	
18	eighteen	
19	nineteen	
20	twenty	

Amusement park

merry-go-round   mat

slide

Ferris wheel

amusement ride

popcorn

ring toss

roller coaster

rifle range   bumper cars   cotton candy

Circus

unicyclist

trapeze

tightrope walker

pole

tightrope

rope ladder

safety net

acrobats

ringmaster

rabbit

dog

top hat

juggler

hoop

bow tie

band

bareback rider

clown

55

Words in order

This is a list of all the words in the pictures. They are in the same order as the alphabet. After each word is a number. This is a page number. On that page, you will find the word and a picture.

a

acrobats, 55
actor, 40
actress, 40
adhesive bandage, 31
airport, 21
alive, 45
alphabet, 29
ambulance, 12
American football, 50
amusement park, 54
amusement ride, 54
antenna, 12
apartments, 13
apple, 30
apricot, 34
apron, 6
aquarium, 29
archery, 51
arm, 38
arrows, 14
artist, 40
astronaut, 40
aunt, 41
autumn, 48
ax, 11

b

baby, 17
baby buggy, 9
back (of body), 38
back (not front), 45
backpack, 20
bad, 44

badge, 29
badger, 22
badminton, 51
bait, 50
baker, 41
ball, 17, 50
balloon, 32
banana, 31
band, 55
bandage, 30
bank, 15
barber, 41
bareback rider, 55
barge, 23
barn, 24
barrel, 11
baseball, 50
basket, 31, 35, 49
basketball, 50
bat (animal), 18
bat (for sport), 50
bathrobe, 30
bathtub, 4
bathroom, 4
battery, 20
beach, 27
beach chair, 27
beads, 14
beak, 49
beans, 35
bear, 18, 19, 30
beaver, 19
bed, 4
bedroom, 5
bee, 9
beehive, 8
belt, 39
bench, 16
bicycle, 13
big, 44
birds, 17
bird's nest, 9
birthday, 47
birthday cake, 47
birthday card, 47
bison, 19

black, 52
blind (for a window),
blow, 43
blue, 52
board, 10, 28
boat, 15, 17, 26, 27
boiled egg, 36
bolts, 11
bone, 9
bonfire, 9
books, 28
boots, 39
bottles, 35
bottom (of body), 38
bottom (not top), 44
bow, 15
bowls, 7
bow tie, 55
box, 29
boy, 28
bread, 33
break, 42
breakfast, 36
bricks, 8, 14
bride, 47
bridegroom, 47
bridesmaid, 47
bridge, 23
broom, 7
brother, 41
brown, 52
brush, 5, 7, 29
bucket, 26
buckle, 39
budgerigar, 49
buffers (train), 20
bulb (light), 33
bull, 24
bulldozer, 12
bumper cars, 54
bus, 12
bus driver, 41
bush, 16
butcher, 40
butter, 33
butterfly, 22

This revised edition first published in 1995 by Usborne Publishing Ltd, Usborne House, 83-85 Saffron Hill, London EC1N 8RT. Based on a previous title first published in 1979. Copyright © 1995, 1979 Usborne Publishing Ltd.